W9-CMZ-966

UBS
TM

Cubs Win! Cubs Win!

Aimee Aryal

Illustrated by Danny Moore

MASCOT BOOKS

www.mascotbooks.com

It was a windy, cold February day in Chicago. *Chicago Cubs* player and team captain, Bradley Moore, was resting comfortably in his warm home near *Wrigley Field*. Bradley was getting ready for his fifteenth—and last—season as the shortstop for the Chicago Cubs.

Growing up in Chicago, Bradley had always dreamed about leading the Cubs to the playoffs and possibly even winning a World Series championship for the North Siders.

All over Chicagoland,
Cubs fans were ready
for the weather to warm
up and for their beloved
Cubbies to start a new season.
On Groundhog Day, Bradley
watched as Punxsutawney Phil saw
his shadow. There would be another
six weeks of winter in the Windy City.

Fortunately for Bradley, he was heading to warm,
sunny Arizona for another Cubs *Spring Training*
and the start of a new baseball season.

Bradley packed his bags and drove to O'Hare Airport. He boarded an airplane and took his seat. The flight attendant immediately recognized the star player. She said, "Go, Cubbies!"

The airplane zoomed down the runway and traveled southwest to Arizona—the Spring Training home of the Chicago Cubs. As Bradley exited the plane, he was surprised to see so many Cubs fans awaiting his arrival. The fans cheered, "Go, Cubbies!"

With a few hours before he needed to report to Spring Training, Bradley decided to play a round of golf in the desert. After a beautiful shot, Bradley's caddie, also a Cubs fan, said, "Go, Cubbies!"

It was finally time for Bradley to report to Chicago Cubs Spring Training at HoHoKam Park in Mesa, Arizona, where he received his uniform and baseball equipment. Excited to see their teammates, Cubs players greeted each other with cheers of, "Go, Cubbies!"

On the field, the players were amazed to see thousands of their adoring fans, each hoping that this would be the magical season they had been waiting for.

The Cubs worked hard during Spring Training. The team practiced baseball skills, like batting, bunting, fielding, and base running. There was also time for some fun, too.

The team played “Rock, Paper, Scissors” and held a bubblegum blowing contest, which Bradley won for the tenth year in a row!

The players loved visiting with the many Cubs fans who had traveled from all over the world to see their beloved team. As a few players rode a golf cart around the ballpark, fans called, “Go, Cubbies!”

As the calendar turned to March, the Cubs played Spring Training games in the *Cactus League*.

On St. Patrick's Day, the team wore special green jerseys to mark the holiday.

Meanwhile, back in Chicago, Chicagoans celebrated the holiday by attending parades all over the city. The Chicago River was turned green, adding to the festive atmosphere. Cubs fans were hoping this was the season their beloved team would enjoy the “Luck o’ the Irish.”

The Cubs returned home to Chicago the first week in April for the start of the season. On Opening Day, Cubs fans bundled up and made their way to historic *Wrigley Field*. Everyone was excited that it was baseball time again.

As each player's
name was called,
they ran from the
Cubs dugout to the
first base line. The players
removed their caps and gazed
at the American Flag for the singing of the
National Anthem.

Cubs fans cheered, "Go, Cubbies!" The umpire
called, "Play Ball!" The season had begun!

As spring turned to summer, the weather warmed and the Chicago Cubs were playing great baseball. On Independence Day, fans arrived to the ballpark to find the Cubs leading the National League Central Division. There was something special about this year's team. Maybe this was the year!

The Cubs played an afternoon game on the Fourth of July at Wrigley Field. Fans, and even some players, dressed in patriotic red, white, and blue. Bradley made a game-saving, spectacular catch to end the game. Another win for the Cubbies!

That night, Cubs players and fans, ventured to Navy Pier, where everyone enjoyed a colorful fireworks display. Bradley sure was proud to be a Cubs player…and an American!

In September, the baseball season was winding down. Thanks to more great baseball, the Cubs won the National League Central Division. September also marked back-to-school time all over Chicagoland.

Bradley loved to go to area elementary schools to talk about baseball and schoolwork. He especially loved reading books to children. Students asked Bradley what it was like to be a professional baseball player and the team captain for the Cubs. When it was time to leave, the whole class cheered, “Go, Cubbies!”

In the playoffs, led by Bradley, the Cubs played more great baseball. The Cubs hit the baseball all over the ballpark and some onto Waveland Avenue. With great pitching and great defense, the team won game-after-game. What a magical season it had been for the team. Everyone cheered, "Go, Cubbies!"

For Bradley, this Chicago Cubs season, his last season with the team, was truly one to remember. He was happy to be part of a history-making team that brought such joy to Cubs fans everywhere.

Walking past *Wrigley Field*, he thought about what a great season it had been and how lucky he was to have played for the Chicago Cubs.

Everywhere Bradley went, Cubs fans cheered, “Go, Cubbies!”

UBS
TM

GO
UBBIES

WRIGLEY FIELD
HOME OF
CHICAGO CUBS
60 DAYS UNTI
OPENING
CHICAGO
CUBS

For Anna and Maya. ~ Aimee Aryal

For my Mom and Pop who made me
what I am today. ~ Danny Moore

For more information about our products,
please visit us online at www.mascotbooks.com.

For more information, please contact Mascot Books,
P.O. Box 220157, Chantilly, VA 20153-0157

ISBN: 1-934878-59-6
CPSIA Code: PRT0510B

Printed in the United States.

www.mascotbooks.com

Baseball

Boston Red Sox	Hello, *Wally*!	Jerry Remy
Boston Red Sox	*Wally The Green Monster* And His Journey Through *Red Sox Nation*!	Jerry Remy
Boston Red Sox	Coast to Coast with *Wally The Green Monster*	Jerry Remy
Boston Red Sox	A Season with *Wally The Green Monster*	Jerry Remy
Colorado Rockies	Hello, *Dinger*!	Aimee Aryal
Detroit Tigers	Hello, *Paws*!	Aimee Aryal
New York Yankees	Let's Go, *Yankees*!	Yogi Berra
New York Yankees	*Yankees* Town	Aimee Aryal
New York Mets	Hello, *Mr. Met*!	Rusty Staub
New York Mets	*Mr. Met* and his Journey Through the Big Apple	Aimee Aryal
St. Louis Cardinals	Hello, *Fredbird*!	Ozzie Smith
Philadelphia Phillies	Hello, *Phillie Phanatic*!	Aimee Aryal
Chicago Cubs	Let's Go, *Cubs*!	Aimee Aryal
Chicago White Sox	Let's Go, *White Sox*!	Aimee Aryal
Cleveland Indians	Hello, *Slider*!	Bob Feller
Seattle Mariners	Hello, *Mariner Moose*!	Aimee Aryal
Washington Nationals	Hello, *Screech*!	Aimee Aryal
Milwaukee Brewers	Hello, *Bernie Brewer*!	Aimee Aryal

College

Alabama	Hello, Big Al!	Aimee Aryal
Alabama	Roll Tide!	Ken Stabler
Alabama	Big Al's Journey Through the Yellowhammer State	Aimee Aryal
Arizona	Hello, Wilbur!	Lute Olson
Arizona State	Hello, Sparky!	Aimee Aryal
Arkansas	Hello, Big Red!	Aimee Aryal
Arkansas	Big Red's Journey Through the Razorback State	Aimee Aryal
Auburn	Hello, Aubie!	Aimee Aryal
Auburn	War Eagle!	Pat Dye
Auburn	Aubie's Journey Through the Yellowhammer State	Aimee Aryal
Boston College	Hello, Baldwin!	Aimee Aryal
Brigham Young	Hello, Cosmo!	LaVell Edwards
Cal - Berkeley	Hello, Oski!	Aimee Aryal
Clemson	Hello, Tiger!	Aimee Aryal
Clemson	Tiger's Journey Through the Palmetto State	Aimee Aryal
Colorado	Hello, Ralphie!	Aimee Aryal
Connecticut	Hello, Jonathan!	Aimee Aryal
Duke	Hello, Blue Devil!	Aimee Aryal
Florida	Hello, Albert!	Aimee Aryal
Florida	Albert's Journey Through the Sunshine State	Aimee Aryal
Florida State	Let's Go, 'Noles!	Aimee Aryal
Georgia	Hello, Hairy Dawg!	Aimee Aryal
Georgia	How 'Bout Them Dawgs!	Vince Dooley
Georgia	Hairy Dawg's Journey Through the Peach State	Vince Dooley
Georgia Tech	Hello, Buzz!	Aimee Aryal
Gonzaga	Spike, The Gonzaga Bulldog	Mike Pringle
Illinois	Let's Go, Illini!	Aimee Aryal
Indiana	Let's Go, Hoosiers!	Aimee Aryal
Iowa	Hello, Herky!	Aimee Aryal
Iowa State	Hello, Cy!	Amy DeLashmutt
James Madison	Hello, Duke Dog!	Aimee Aryal
Kansas	Hello, Big Jay!	Aimee Aryal
Kansas State	Hello, Willie!	Dan Walter
Kentucky	Hello, Wildcat!	Aimee Aryal
LSU	Hello, Mike!	Aimee Aryal
LSU	Mike's Journey Through the Bayou State	Aimee Aryal
Maryland	Hello, Testudo!	Aimee Aryal
Michigan	Let's Go, Blue!	Aimee Aryal
Michigan State	Hello, Sparty!	Aimee Aryal
Michigan State	Sparty's Journey Through Michigan	Aimee Aryal
Middle Tennessee	Hello, Lightning!	Aimee Aryal
Minnesota	Hello, Goldy!	Aimee Aryal
Mississippi	Hello, Colonel Rebel!	Aimee Aryal

Pro Football

Carolina Panthers	Let's Go, Panthers!	Aimee Aryal
Chicago Bears	Let's Go, Bears!	Aimee Aryal
Dallas Cowboys	How 'Bout Them Cowboys!	Aimee Aryal
Green Bay Packers	Go, Pack, Go!	Aimee Aryal
Kansas City Chiefs	Let's Go, Chiefs!	Aimee Aryal
Minnesota Vikings	Let's Go, Vikings!	Aimee Aryal
New York Giants	Let's Go, Giants!	Aimee Aryal
New York Jets	J-E-T-S! Jets, Jets, Jets!	Aimee Aryal
New England Patriots	Let's Go, Patriots!	Aimee Aryal
Pittsburg Steelers	Here We Go, Steelers!	Aimee Aryal
Seattle Seahawks	Let's Go, Seahawks!	Aimee Aryal
Washington Redskins	Hail To The Redskins!	Aimee Aryal

Basketball

Dallas Mavericks	Let's Go, Mavs!	Mark Cuban
Boston Celtics	Let's Go, Celtics!	Aimee Aryal

Other

Kentucky Derby	White Diamond Runs For The Roses	Aimee Aryal
Marine Corps Marathon	Run, Miles, Run!	Aimee Aryal

Mississippi State	Hello, Bully!	Aimee Aryal
Missouri	Hello, Truman!	Todd Donoho
Missouri	Hello, Truman! Show Me Missouri!	Todd Donoho
Nebraska	Hello, Herbie Husker!	Aimee Aryal
North Carolina	Hello, Rameses!	Aimee Aryal
North Carolina	Rameses' Journey Through the Tar Heel State	Aimee Aryal
North Carolina St.	Hello, Mr. Wuf!	Aimee Aryal
North Carolina St.	Mr. Wuf's Journey Through North Carolina	Aimee Aryal
Northern Arizona	Hello, Louie!	Jeanette S. Baker
Notre Dame	Let's Go, Irish!	Aimee Aryal
Ohio State	Hello, Brutus!	Aimee Aryal
Ohio State	Brutus' Journey	Aimee Aryal
Oklahoma	Let's Go, Sooners!	Aimee Aryal
Oklahoma State	Hello, Pistol Pete!	Aimee Aryal
Oregon	Go Ducks!	Aimee Aryal
Oregon State	Hello, Benny the Beaver!	Aimee Aryal
Penn State	Hello, Nittany Lion!	Aimee Aryal
Penn State	We Are Penn State!	Joe Paterno
Purdue	Hello, Purdue Pete!	Aimee Aryal
Rutgers	Hello, Scarlet Knight!	Aimee Aryal
South Carolina	Hello, Cocky!	Aimee Aryal
South Carolina	Cocky's Journey Through the Palmetto State	Aimee Aryal
So. California	Hello, Tommy Trojan!	Aimee Aryal
Syracuse	Hello, Otto!	Aimee Aryal
Tennessee	Hello, Smokey!	Aimee Aryal
Tennessee	Smokey's Journey Through the Volunteer State	Aimee Aryal
Texas	Hello, Hook 'Em!	Aimee Aryal
Texas	Hook 'Em's Journey Through the Lone Star State	Aimee Aryal
Texas A & M	Howdy, Reveille!	Aimee Aryal
Texas A & M	Reveille's Journey Through the Lone Star State	Aimee Aryal
Texas Tech	Hello, Masked Rider!	Aimee Aryal
UCLA	Hello, Joe Bruin!	Aimee Aryal
Virginia	Hello, CavMan!	Aimee Aryal
Virginia Tech	Hello, Hokie Bird!	Aimee Aryal
Virginia Tech	Yea, It's Hokie Game Day!	Frank Beamer
Virginia Tech	Hokie Bird's Journey Through Virginia	Aimee Aryal
Wake Forest	Hello, Demon Deacon!	Aimee Aryal
Washington	Hello, Harry the Husky!	Aimee Aryal
Washington State	Hello, Butch!	Aimee Aryal
West Virginia	Hello, Mountaineer!	Aimee Aryal
West Virginia	The Mountaineer's Journey Through West Virginia	Leslie H. Haning
Wisconsin	Hello, Bucky!	Aimee Aryal
Wisconsin	Bucky's Journey Through the Badger State	Aimee Aryal

Order online at **mascotbooks.com** using promo code " **free**" to receive **FREE SHIPPING!**

More great titles coming soon!

info@mascotbooks.com

CHICAGO
CUBS
TM

UBS
TM